Firebird

Linda Winstead Jones

To Lauren,

Best Wishes!

Linda Winstead Jones

Firebird, Copyright 2014 by Linda Winstead Jones.
Print Edition, 2014

ISBN-13: 978-1495292439
ISBN-10: 1495292436

Cover design by Elizabeth Wallace
http://designwithin.carbonmade.com/

Print Design by A Thirsty Mind Book Design
http://www.athirstymind.com/

Chapter One

The air felt different here, so very far from the Anwyn Mountains Rori had called home for all of her twenty-three years. There was a tang in that air that she'd already become accustomed to; that she'd somehow come to need. Alone on a long stretch of the beach, she watched the waves rise and break. The blue-green water seemed to go on forever, stretching to the horizon and beyond. It was at once a soothing and terrifying sight. The ocean reminded her that the world beyond her home was vast, with unexplored corners and strange people and dangers she'd never even dreamed of.

Not that she would ever travel beyond these shores. Though she was occasionally tempted to get on a ship and sail away, she never would. This seaside village was as far as she cared, or dared, to go.

Yes, everything was different here. The warm sand beneath her bare feet and between her toes; massive rocks to the north and to the south which reminded her of the mountains of home and yet were craggier, sharper; sea birds which were unlike any other bird she'd seen before moving here. Comforting scents wafted from the small village she intended to make her new home, scents which were faint as she stood so close to the sea. Her enhanced Anwyn sense of smell detected baking bread, blooming flowers, sweat, and sunshine on the stone pathways. There were less pleasant odors, of course, but she ignored those and concentrated on the scents she liked.

Rori had so many cousins it was almost impossible to travel ten miles in Columbyana without tripping over one, or more. To her knowledge, none had traveled this far east. She was safe here, at the edge of the world.

"I am not lonely," she whispered. "I do not miss my family." Maybe if she said the words often enough she would eventually take them to heart.

Rori did have occasional doubts about her rash decision, but she knew in her heart that leaving home had been her only option. She was an embarrassment to her family. A freak. Twenty-three years old, and her mate had not appeared. Maybe he was dead. Maybe he knew her secret and was ashamed to claim her.

Then again, it was possible that no mate was destined to be hers, that she was like her father's Caradon ancestors, wild and free mountain cat shifters who refused to be tied down by any bonds. She loved her father very much; he was a fine man who loved his wife and his children. But that didn't mean Rori wanted to be like her paternal ancestors. *Wild and free* might agree with some, but it was not what Rori wanted from life.

She wanted love.

Her sisters had all been claimed by Anwyn mates, males of their mother's people who lived in The City or just beyond, men who had carried them off when the time was right. Kidnapping was the custom, but then an Anwyn male's mates were usually human. Beyond her family, female-born Anwyn were rare. In the case of her sisters, the males had wisely gone to the King and Queen to ask permission before taking their daughters into the mountains. They valued their heads.

No one had ever come for Rori, with or without permission.

It didn't matter why no one had claimed her. For many reasons, there was no place for her in the Anwyn Mountains. Daughter of a Queen and a fire-starting Caradon King, Granddaughter of a Fyne witch who was undoubtedly the most powerful shifter the Anwyn had ever known, and she…

She did not wish to think about it. The village she'd chosen as her new home was so far from the pull of the Anwyn Mountains she need never shift again, though twice since coming here she'd been drawn out by the full moon and had allowed herself to transform. No more, though. If the desire came again she would fight it. Here she could leave behind the girl she'd once been and become a normal woman. With her gifts as a healer and the valuable possessions she'd brought with her to her new home, she could live very happily in this village by the sea.

And she would not live alone. When the time came she would take a human husband. She would have children. Wild and free? Never.

Rori turned her back on the Cardean Ocean and walked toward her rented cottage. Her new home was small and the exterior—a mixture of stone and mortar and wood—was weathered by the sea air and the occasional fearsome winds that blew in off the ocean, but it had been very well built. It was a peaceful place, with two spacious rooms, a welcoming red door, vines heavy with roses, and—from her bedroom window—a view of the ocean she'd come to love and fear. It was not at all like the palace where she'd lived her first twenty-three years, a palace with massive rooms that had been cut deep into the mountain. That was home for an Anwyn princess; this was home for the woman she wished to be.

As Rori reached the door to her cottage, she paused. The back of her neck tingled; her fingers trembled. She was almost certain someone was watching her. Did she dare turn to look? Had her mother's guards found her?

That strange feeling was just her imagination, she decided with finality. No one watched. No one would ever find her here.

She never knew what the day would bring. The only other healer in the area lived a good distance away from the village proper, and was not very welcoming, from all Rori had heard. Thanks to a variety of ordinary ailments, she stayed busy. She might see a child with a runny nose in the morning and a deathly ill elderly person in the afternoon. Most came to her looking for healing, but at times she walked to the home of a very ill person, if they were unable to make their way to her. She treated injuries and illnesses of all sorts, and payment came in the way of bread, eggs, produce, flowers, and fish, along with the occasional coin. Some days were busier than others, but she had not been bored or idle since coming here.

Unlike her grandmother, her healing was not of the magical sort. She'd learned about herbs and poultices from Juliet Fyne, who'd sensed a talent in her youngest granddaughter. There were times when she wished she could heal with a touch, but she could not.

By the time the sun set she was almost always exhausted. It was her ritual to prepare a simple dinner, bathe, and fall into bed to sleep.

She'd been in this village for more than three months now, and during that time she'd dreamed of a man—a particular man—several times. In the dream they might be in the same strange room, or on the same hill, or in the same forest. He was just *there*, silent and apart and yet still close to her in a way she could not explain. It was as if she was so aware of his presence that her entire body tingled in fear and anticipation. Anticipation of what, she did not know.

At first she'd been afraid, had awakened from her dreams in a cold sweat. Was he a danger or a friend? A real man or a product of her imagination?

In the past ten days those dreams had changed. They came every night, and were so much more vivid than before.

She didn't know the man's name and she never remembered his face. And yet, even after waking he seemed almost real. So warm, so powerful. When she woke it was as if she missed her dream man with an unnatural intensity. Each morning she tried to remember more, and day by day the image in her mind became clearer.

He was a large man with dark hair and many muscles. His eyes were dark, his jaw strong. He was very tall and, she decided, not a danger to her after all.

For each of the past five nights, he'd moved closer to her. Around trees that grew tall between them; across a room packed with strangers; down a grassy hill. He came so close she could almost touch him. As he approached her heart raced, her breath would hardly come, her entire body trembled. Still, even in her dream she understood that she would never know him, would never truly touch him. Real or imagined he was just a dream, and that realization broke her heart.

Tonight her dream man finally reached her. He towered above her. He did not speak, but she could hear him breathing. She felt the warmth rolling off his body. He seemed so real, not a dream at all. Following her instincts she removed his shirt and raked her fingers across his warm skin. Heaven above, he was so much larger than she was! Taller, wider, he all but blocked the sun as he towered over her. *Sun.* Tonight's dream had taken her to a beach much like the one beyond her bedroom window. They were alone. No fishermen were nearby, no children ran and played in the sand. The beach was just for her and her nameless man.

He leaned down, and with his nose in her hair he inhaled deeply, slowly. When he exhaled he whispered, speaking to her at last.

"I'm coming for you."

Just a dream, Rori reminded herself as her heart skipped a beat.

"You won't find me." No one would find her here. She'd come too far, planned too well.

There was always desire in her dreams of this man, but that desire had never been as powerful as it was at this moment. Dream or not, she wanted him. On the sand, with the sun beating down upon them. She wanted, *needed* him inside her. Maybe her dream lover was the only one she would ever know. Maybe the husband and family she desired were nothing more than another dream. A fantasy.

"Make love to me," she whispered.

He nuzzled her hair, pulled her body against his, held her tight and kissed her neck with fabulous, talented lips. And then he whispered, "No."

Rori pulled away in frustration. "This is my dream, and you will do as I command."

With a smile and a wink he vanished, leaving her on the beach all alone. Rori looked toward the ocean. A storm was coming.

She woke with no memory of the man's face, but she did remember the sensation of his arms around her, and she recalled very vividly the way his lips had felt on her neck. Most annoyingly of all, between her legs she ached in a way she never had before.

There was no going back to sleep after that. She tried for a while, but she could not shake the sensation that he was somehow still with her. Close, as he had been when they'd searched for one another in large rooms and thickly treed forests. *Ridiculous.* He was not real! Rori left her bed, pulled on a wrapper, and wandered into the main room to light the fire. She'd prepare a pot of tea and rearrange her shelf of herbs to pass the time. She'd make notes on the patients she'd seen this week. She never knew when she might have to refer back to another illness in order to make sense of a new one.

By the time the sun rose she'd made numerous notes and had reorganized her shelf of herbs twice. She kept looking at those herbs, wondering what sort of potion she might make for herself to ease this new pain. A tonic to kill her desire for a man she would never know. Perhaps she had a bit of the Anwyn in her, after all. When her sisters were fertile they were demanding and short-tempered. Did they *want* this way? Had they been almost mad with desire? If she'd known, she might have been more sympathetic.

Fertile. She was an unmarried woman making a new life in a small, provincial village. If she wished to remain here for a lifetime, if she wished to find a proper husband, it would be best if she didn't indulge her instincts each time they flared to life. A potion to kill the desire, to end the dreams…surely that could be done. She brushed her fingers over a bottle or two, then dropped them. Not now. Not yet. Even if he wasn't real, she didn't want to give up her dream lover so soon.

Far from the pull of home, shifting did not come easily to Kalum. But the moon was full, and he was stronger than most. After the frustrating shared dream he needed to run, to push himself, to answer the primitive call of the Caradon. When he was panther he did not think, and he did not hurt. There was only the night, and the moon, and the power.

Near dawn he took his human form. Naked again, man again, from a gently sloped green hill he looked to the east. The sun shone in his eyes, making the village shimmer as if it were not real. But it was real, and she was there.

The Caradon did not mate for life, as the Anwyn did. Rori's father was the exception, a necessary aberration. Everyone knew the story. Joryn's joining with the Anwyn queen had been necessary to bring peace to their people. Their marriage had been foretold, but it certainly had not changed the ways of the Caradon.

Which is why Kalum's lifelong dreams of an Anwyn princess had been so incredibly annoying. He'd moved away from the Mountains of the North, he'd tried to lose himself in endeavors which might take his mind off of this woman he should not want. Nothing had worked. She was his, and like it or not, he needed her.

For more than a week he'd watched and waited. He'd planned. He'd dreamed. He'd dreamed of *her*.

And he whispered into the wind. "I'm coming for you."

Chapter Two

Her first patient of the day was an infant, who came through Rori's door cradled in the arms of his worried mother. The poor child had been crying half the night for the past several days. Rori made a gentle tonic for the baby, who was teething early, and a stronger tea for the mother, who was on the verge of exhaustion.

The day continued as usual, until a very pretty woman arrived. Rori had not seen the woman in town, but that in itself was not alarming. There were many small farms inland and fishing villages up and down the coast. There were goat herders who lived on the gentlest hills, and a family who worked in iron just west of those hills. She didn't know everyone along the eastern seaboard, and she never would.

Rori was certain she would have remembered this woman, if they'd crossed paths in the past. Her newest patient had long dark hair, vivid green eyes, and skin like milk. Tall and thin, she moved with an unusual grace, as if the feet hidden beneath her too-long black skirt did not always touch the ground. Her clothing was worn, plain in both color and in design, which was in sharp contrast to her elegance and the softness of her skin and her hands. The young woman wasn't just pretty, she was striking. Perhaps even unforgettably so.

The nervous young woman—Rori judged that she was likely close to her own age—perched on a chair and looked down into her lap. Rori asked a few questions but the woman refused to give a name, refused to tell where she lived.

Perhaps she was pregnant and unmarried. Or had an illness she was ashamed of. Maybe she was simply very shy. Or…good heavens, she was not psychic. Two of her sisters, yes, but not her. The woman would have to tell her what was wrong, no matter what it might be.

"How can I help you?"

The pretty woman lifted her head and stared at Rori with desperate eyes that seemed to flash an unnatural green, they were so bright.

"I hear you're a very powerful healer."

"I do what I can," Rori said, more curious than ever. None of her current patients had come to her asking about *power*. "But I have no magic, if that is what you seek."

The disappointment that washed over the woman's face was almost painful to see. "I don't know what I seek. I just want someone, anyone, to fix me." The desperation in her voice was unmistakable.

If only it was so easy. Rori dismissed her thought that she herself would love to be *fixed* and returned her attention to her patient. "What's wrong?"

The woman looked back at the red door as if she was already sorry she'd come through it. Rori half expected her to bolt out of the room, but she did not. After a long, dejected sigh she said, "I was born twenty years ago to a fisherman's wife. My father was not the fisherman. The soldiers who raided the village killed him, Mama said."

"I'm very sorry," Rori whispered. It was a hard way to come into the world. And then she did the math in her head. *Twenty years.* Was it possible? Was she…one of *them*?

There was only one way to find out. "Your father was possessed by the demon?"

"Yes." The answer was so soft if there had been a whisper of a breeze in the room it would have whisked it away.

"You are one of the demon's daughters." The war

had already begun in small pockets of the country. The capital city of Arthes was constantly under siege, and the western border of Columbyana and into Tryfyn was not at all safe. Even to the south, near the gulf, it was rumored that many Ksana demons had gathered to do their worst. War had not yet touched the mountains Rori had once called home, or the village that was becoming her new home, but there were frightened whispers from those who feared it was coming to all corners of the known world.

The residents of this village had a legend which promised a creature that would protect them from such dangers. A rather scrawny dragon had been painted and carved on many doors and walls and signs. The depictions which could be seen about town were not identical, but there were some similarities. The body was thinner than most mythical drawings she'd seen, and the tail sported as many feathers as it did scales. There was always fire, of course.

Rori suspected the villagers would be mightily disappointed if war did come here and no dragon rose from the seaside bluffs to save them. Dragons had been gone from this world for a very long time.

Fear had not yet taken hold of the village, but they were not ignorant of the troubles to the west. There were those who would kill this woman on sight if they knew she was one of the demon's daughters. No matter what she'd done or had not done.

"Can you fix me?" the poor girl whispered. "Is there a medicine that will take away that part of myself?"

"I don't know. Your will is strong. Your desire not to give in to…"

"Is often enough," the woman snapped. "And sometimes is not. It's as if he speaks to me, as if the demon lives inside me and whispers into my mind when I least expect it. His voice is getting stronger, louder. I have not slept for days." The demon daughter cocked her head, and while she was still beautiful, she no longer looked at all innocent. "He wants me to do terrible things. I have done as he commands in the past, but I want it to end. I want to be normal."

Normal. She could empathize.

"I'll see what I can do," Rori said. She wasn't sure where to start, but she had several old books she could study. If only her grandmother were here! Former Queen Juliet would be a great help in this situation. Unfortunately, if Juliet knew where her granddaughter had gone soon her daughter, the current Queen, would also know.

Her mother and grandmother were both very psychic. Thank goodness their powers to see did not extend to those closest to them. They would be all but blind where Rori was concerned. If not, this little village would have been swarming with Queen's Guards weeks ago.

"Come back in three days," Rori said, standing to indicate that the consultation was over.

The nameless woman stood and nodded, then walked toward the door. With her fingers resting lightly on the door handle, she turned to look at Rori. "You have more power than you know."

Rori shook her head. Power? Quite the opposite.

"You may call me Lucia."

For a moment Rori wondered if that was the woman's real name, but she quickly decided it didn't matter. "Thank you. I will."

Before Lucia left she had one more thing to say.

"You have fire, like your father."

Kalum watched from a distance as Rori left her cottage and walked toward the ocean, as she'd done for the past three afternoons. Perhaps that was her routine. He growled under his breath. It was foolish for a Queen's daughter to have a routine. There were always those who would like to profit from kidnapping or take revenge by harming a beloved child.

His mate had magnificent reddish brown hair and unusual blue eyes with just a few small but brilliant specks of gold. All Anwyn had eyes some shade of gold, just as all Caradon had eyes of green. He could not see those eyes from this distance, but he'd dreamed about them often. He wondered if they were truly blue, and if they were, if they were as blue as they'd been in his dreams. He could hardly wait to see. There were many things he could hardly wait for.

The dress she wore was much like the others he'd seen on her. Plain, but well-made. Soft, elegant. Rori wore clothing made for a princess, though she seemed to be unaware of that fact. Did she not note that her patients wore much rougher materials, and some of them possessed only one decent suit of clothes? Did she not know that the fabrics on her body screamed that she was not like other women?

A part of him wanted to run to the beach, grab her, and carry her into the nearby hills to make her his in every way. He wanted to kidnap her, as was the way of Anwyn males and their mates. But he was not a fool, and he was not Anwyn. He would get more from Rori if he moved slowly. If he wooed her.

Wooing was not the way of the Anwyn *or* the Caradon, but this situation was unique. Unique, hell, it was groundbreaking.

Though he'd denied Rori for years, had turned away from the inescapable fact that they were mated, destined as her parents and so many of the Anwyn had been, he had finally accepted the truth. To live without her would eventually drive him mad. She might not realize it yet, but madness would claim her, too. In time.

A few nights in her bed would ease his suffering and

put an end to the dreams. At least for a while. Perhaps they would spend a lifetime coming together and moving apart. Perhaps this one time would be enough to ease the pain. It wasn't as if he could present such an offer to her. She was an Anwyn princess after all, and a crude offer of release would not get him where he needed to be.

Her bed.

He walked toward her, basket in hand. He'd observed the fishermen in the village for the past several days. His clothes and demeanor were appropriately simple, but his heart was pounding so hard he was afraid she might hear it, even from a distance.

Apparently she did not hear his heartbeat or his approach. Her attention was on the waves, the sea, the endlessness of it. He could tell that she was not aware of him until he stood beside her. Close, but not too close. If he touched her, she might know who he was and why he was here. Did she realize her dreams were, to some extent, shared? Did she know her mate had come for her?

"It's amazing, isn't it?" he said, placing his basket of fish on the sand.

Startled, she turned her head to look at him. He looked back. Those eyes were magnificent, even more arresting than they'd been in his dreams. A more vibrant blue, with flecks of gold that sparked. "Yes," she said. "Amazing."

With that she dismissed him, turning her attention once more to the sea.

"I've lived here for years." Kalum looked upon the waves as she did, and delivered the lie. After all, he wanted her to think of him as she would any other man. "And this view still takes my breath away."

She did not say anything to extend the conversation. Nothing at all.

"My name's Kalum," he said. "I live just to the south of the village." He gave her a moment to respond, but she did not. So he prodded, "And you are?"

"Not interested," she said sharply.

He laughed, and judging by the expression on her face his response surprised her. He'd known for years that she would not be easy. "I'm not flirting with you, I'm simply being friendly."

She sighed. "Fine. My name's Rori, I live in the village, and I'm a healer."

"Was that so hard?" he teased.

"Your fish stink." Her response was soft and annoyed and dismissive.

"That they do."

"Perhaps you should hurry along home before they spoil."

"Perhaps I should." But he did not move. She would soon head back to her home, leaving him standing here with an awe inspiring view and stinking fish. And next time he got close to her she would move away before he had a chance to speak. He'd never attempted to woo any woman before this, and so far he was a failure. The Caradon were not meant to *woo*.

Maybe he should have simply presented her with the truth. He'd been so sure that would frighten or alarm her, he'd decided to get to know her in a more normal fashion. Since he'd already begun, it was too late to change his approach now.

"You're a beautiful woman and I have no wife as of yet. Would you give me permission to call on you, Rori the healer?"

"No!" With that response and a withering glance, she turned and walked away. She might have stalked away, but stalking was impossible in the shifting sands.

He watched and smiled. Rori had the regal and graceful walk of a queen's daughter. The power of a shifter. And there was so much sensuality in that walk that observing her departure made him hard.

Perhaps their initial meeting had not gone as he'd planned, but one way or another he would have her. She'd give in to the instincts that were sure to draw her to him just as he was drawn to her. Soon, he hoped.

The dream was unlike any other. Her dream lover touched her as he never had before. He laid his lips over hers; his hand delved between her legs. Rori moaned and then she asked for more. She begged him to take her.

And again, he said no.

He whispered in her ear. "If you want me, you must come to me in the flesh."

"I can't."

"You can."

She sounded desperate; he sounded smug.

She could and would seduce him. It was her dream, after all. *Her* dream, which meant she was frustrating herself.

Rori shook off her frustration and went after her dream lover. She placed a hand on the ridge beneath his trousers. He could deny it, but he *did* want her. That much was quite clear. She raked her hand up along his erection and then stopped, allowing her palm to rest over and against it. She wiggled her fingers; he growled, just a little. Reluctantly, she left behind the impressive indicator of his desire to unbutton his shirt. The linen was quickly discarded, and when he was bare chested she began to kiss his chest, his flat nipples, his ridged torso. Oh, the muscles! They were so very fine.

His breathing changed, his body stiffened. Her seduction was working. She smiled, raked her tongue from one nipple to his navel and just below.

Tell me no now.

As if he'd read her mind, he backed away and said

that dreaded word. *No.*

"You can't deny who you are by running to the other side of the world," he said as he took another step back.

"Yes, I can!" Rori snapped.

"No. You need me. I need you. And neither of us belongs here."

Her breath caught, her heart pounded. This was more than a dream. Much more. Her dream lover was her *mate.* He was more than a dream, he was *real.* His eyes were a very dark green, she finally noted, marking him as a Caradon. *No, no, no.* Another way she was different. Another failing. All Caradon males were uncivilized beasts! With her father as the exception, of course.

"If you are who you claim to be, you're late!" she snapped.

"You should have waited for me to go to The City. Why did you run away? Why did you leave?"

She wouldn't say, not even in a dream that was evidently more than a dream.

He turned, and for the first time she noted the tattoo on his right shoulder. It was a winged something, though she could not tell exactly what. The wings made her shudder. Did he know? Had he seen more in his dreams than she wanted him to see?

No, if he knew the truth he would not want her. He would be satisfied with his life as an unwed, unmated Caradon. He could lie with other women, as all Caradon heathens did.

Could she do the same? Could she lie with other men? Why not? She was not like the others, not like her sisters or her mother or her grandmother, so rules should not apply to her. Oh, that thought was so unlike her. Desire had muddled her brain. Maybe she should find that proper husband she desired sooner rather than later.

"Fine!" she snapped. "Walk away. If you're not going to lie with me then don't bother coming back!"

He glanced over his shoulder and smiled. "You only want me for my cock, eh?"

"I don't want you at all!"

He continued to smile. "Liar."

When she woke Rori sat up in the bed and screamed in frustration. Her blankets and nightgown were twisted, her pillow was on the floor by the window. Her dreams had never been like this before. So real. So maddening. Her body ached, her insides trembled with need.

If there was truth in her dreams, she *did* have a mate. And he was Caradon. No, that could not be true.

She did not want a Caradon mate, which would be worse than having no mate at all. Though there had been peace among the Anwyn and the Caradon since her parents had married, the two peoples were hardly on friendly terms.

If there was truth in her dreams her mate, her dream lover, was trying to convince her to return home by denying her physical relief even as she slept. She wasn't doing this to herself; it was a shared dream, and he was all but insisting that she come to him if she wanted his touch. Well, she'd show him. Her Caradon was not the only one who could ease her frustration. There were other men in this village who would do just as well. Better, in fact.

Her mind immediately went to the fisherman she'd met on the beach, the one who had asked if he could call on her. Kalum, that was his name. He was handsome, strong, and had flashed a very pleasant smile in her direction. Not that she required such attributes. In a darkened room, even the ugliest man would do just as well as a pretty one.

Rori wrinkled her nose. Perhaps that was true, but she wanted beauty. She wanted strength. If she was going to indulge in pleasures of the flesh she might as well have it all.

She should've been friendlier when Kalum had spoken to her. At the very least, she should not have snapped at him. Between her disturbing dreams and Lucia's problems she'd been horribly distracted, and his fish truly *had* stunk horribly to her sensitive nose. She hadn't been thinking at all about a chance encounter with a man who might turn out to be the ordinary husband she planned to take, one day.

Plans had a way of going awry; and there were distractions everywhere she turned. All things considered, the fisherman Kalum might do very nicely…

Chapter Three

Kalum was connected to his mate in a way she'd not yet discovered. She would, one day, if she allowed herself to give in to her instincts. But at this moment he had an advantage. He couldn't read her thoughts, he didn't know all, but there were some segments of her mind that all but screamed at him.

She was under the mistaken impression that he could be replaced with any man. He saw that in her, *on* her, as she walked onto the sand once again. Her strides were confident and her eyes remained fixed and determined as she moved unerringly toward him. Yes, he knew very well what she wanted.

He saw so much of her. Not all, not the secret that had compelled her to take up residence so far from home, but he saw much.

Yesterday she'd been annoyed by him. Today she smiled as she walked toward him. Today, she was not at all annoyed. Yet.

"Kalum, isn't it?" she asked when she was near.

"Yes, Rori." Today he was the one who remained cool. After all, she'd rebuffed him once. No self-respecting man would willingly offer himself up for more abuse from a pretty woman who was so obviously uninterested in his advances.

"I'm afraid I was rather rude to you yesterday," she said. "I was distracted by the unusual illness of a patient I'd just met. Please forgive me."

He bowed to her almost formally. "Of course, you are forgiven."

"Perhaps you'll allow me to make amends by preparing you a meal. A woman with a sick child paid me in lamb stew, and there's far more than I need."

Lamb stew and a bedding, that was her plan. She thought she could ease her suffering and end the dreams with any convenient male. He was furious that she would cheat on him, that she would turn her back on her mate to lie with another man. Even if that other man was himself.

"Thank you but no. I have fish for supper, and do not care for lamb."

"Oh." It was clear she hadn't expected to be rebuffed. A beautiful lady, a man who had already expressed an interest…she was not prepared to hear no from him. "Well, perhaps another time."

"Perhaps."

She turned to the ocean, pursing her lips in displeasure. He could almost see her mind spinning. Her initial plan, which he imagined she'd thought to be foolproof, had failed. Apparently she did not have another plan at the ready.

Finally she said, "You did ask just yesterday if you could call on me. Perhaps a stroll…"

"No, thank you. I have walked enough today."

She glanced at him, squinted. Pursed her lips. Gone was the genial and flirtatious girl. "I see. You're angry because I turned you down yesterday."

"I'm not at all angry." To prove it, he smiled. "Have a lovely evening." With that he turned and walked away from her. He could feel her gaze on his back, and was so very tempted to turn and look at her again. But he didn't.

She was still staring when he began to whistle like a man who didn't have a care in the world.

* * * *

Rori turned and strode back toward her cottage. Her life as a princess in The City had not prepared her for rejection. She was accustomed to getting what she wanted, always. Instantly. That was not her life now, she reminded herself. She had wished for a normal life and that was what she had. Normal meant not always getting exactly what she wanted, she supposed.

She could not stand another night of frustrating dreams that left her trembling and aching. She did *not* want to be alone tonight! As she approached her red door she looked down the street. A few people were about, some visiting on a lovely afternoon, others hard at work. Until this moment she had not realized how few single and appropriate men lived in this small village. How could she ever hope to find a husband here?

She needed to find a man more forgiving than Kalum had proved to be. Thinking of him elicited a soft, low snort of derision. Yes, he was handsome, but she needed more. Perhaps it was a good thing that she'd been so distracted when she'd first met him. Best to find out now that he was…difficult.

After a few frustrating moments her eyes fell on a man from a nearby farm who was making deliveries, as he did several times a week.

Ben Skrewd was not a vision of manliness like the fisherman Kalum, but he *was* a man. Unmarried, under thirty years of age, pleasant enough in manner and appearance. His hair was an ordinary brown, as were his eyes. His build was slender. He did stammer on occasion and his nose was uncommonly long, but she didn't want him to talk all that much, and it wasn't as if his nose was misshapen. It was just…long. Rori turned away from her cottage and walked toward Ben, her head high. She was determined to get what she wanted, what she *needed*, even if she wasn't going to get it from the man she'd initially planned upon using.

"Hello, Ben," she called when she was near.

Ben was startled easily, almost jumping out of his skin as he turned to face her. In his large, rough hands he held a box of produce, yet to be delivered. Cabbages, carrots, and onions, she noted. Several feet away his wagon was filled with such boxes.

He stammered a bit before he managed to say, "Hello, Rori. Do you…do you need some…some vegetables? Eggs? Pork?"

No wonder he was not yet married if coming face to face with a woman caused his tongue to tangle and his cheeks to flush such a bright pink.

"No. I just wanted to say hello, and to ask if you had plans for dinner."

An unmarried man who lived alone and worked all day, he would probably be quite happy to have a hot meal, and more, at the end of the day.

"I have no plans." He looked very suspicious. His cheeks remained overly pink.

Rori smiled at him. "I have lamb stew…"

It was torture, to be so close and not have her, to know she wanted and needed him and yet at the same time…

The man walking toward Rori's cottage was not what Kalum would call a fine specimen of the human male. Skinny, pointed nose, feet and hands too large for his body. His pants were an inch or two too short, and his shirt was buttoned all the way to his throat. It looked as if that last button might be choking him a bit. His hair had been slicked back with some kind of grease, and in his big, rough hands he held a sad bouquet of yellow flowers.

Kalum stepped out of his hiding place between two

buildings and approached the man he'd heard Rori call Ben.

"Hello," he said in the friendliest voice he could muster. "You're Ben, yes?"

Ben stopped. One of the yellow flowers wilted, as if it knew what was coming. "Good evening. Pardon me, but do I know you?"

"No, not yet." Kalum moved in close, stifling the urge to throttle this man here and now. Nothing had happened and nothing *would* happen. There was no need for throttling. "You're going to see Rori." It was a statement, not a question, but Ben nodded his head in response.

"Yes, yes I am. Do you know her?"

"I do know her, and I just wanted to offer a friendly warning."

Ben backed up a step. "What kind of warning?"

"Touch her, lay so much as a finger on her, and I will rip you to shreds and use your bones as toothpicks."

Ben paled. He even shook a little. "I have no intention of…of…I'm just having dinner with her, that's all. We're friends, nothing more."

As if this little man could resist Rori if she set her mind to having him. As if this worm would have the strength to look into those blue eyes and tell her no. "Toothpicks," Kalum whispered.

Ben dropped the sad bouquet in the street, turned, and ran. He ran fast, and away from the cottage with the red door. He'd hitched his horse before a shop a few buildings down. Within seconds he was on that horse, leaving town at breakneck speed.

Kalum rescued the flowers from the ground, studied them, and then tossed them aside. One did not present a princess with ragged flowers which were no better than weeds.

He turned, straightened his shirt, and walked toward

the cottage. Perhaps one should not leave a princess waiting and wanting, either.

Rori opened the door, a wide smile plastered on her face. That smile died when she saw the man standing there.

"It's *you*."

"I changed my mind about that stew."

She did not back away from the door and invite Kalum in, even though he looked very nice. He'd dressed in what appeared to be his best clothes, and today he did not stink of fish. Still...

"I'm afraid I've already invited someone else for stew."

"Skinny fellow? Pointy nose?"

She withdrew a bit, surprised. "How do you know Ben?"

Oh, he looked so smug! "I'm afraid your friend Ben won't be here."

"Why not?" she snapped.

Kalum leaned in and down. "I scared him away."

She was so tempted to slam the door in his face! Arrogant jerk. But she did not slam the door. Kalum was handsome, looking at him made her skin tingle and her toes curl in a way that was completely foreign to her and not at all unpleasant, and he was *here*. Maybe he had walked away just a few hours ago, but he was here now.

"I do wish you would make up your mind," she said, trying to sound cool and a little disinterested. "First you ask to call on me, then you rebuff my simple invitation for dinner, and then you scare away my suitor. Do you want to court me or not?"

His voice was deep and smooth and made her shiver just a little when he said, "Courting is not exactly what I have in mind, but then it's not really what you have in mind, either. Is it?"

She was a horrible liar, always had been, so she didn't even try to lie to the big man who stood in her doorway. What she was suffering from was quite natural among her people. She needed a man in her bed. Even this annoying one would do. "I suppose you should come inside," she said coolly.

Rori opened the door wider and moved aside to allow Kalum into her home. He looked even bigger there, confined by the walls of her small home.

"Is there actually lamb stew?"

"Of course," she said, managing to sound at least a little bit indignant.

"I wasn't lying when I said I don't really like lamb," he said, looking around the room that served as clinic, kitchen, and living area.

"Neither do I," she confessed.

His perusal ended and he gave her his full attention. "I assume there is a bed beyond that door?"

She should act shocked and insulted, she supposed, but instead she just nodded. There was power in Kalum's gaze, heat and passion and promise. Great promise. Her heart-rate increased and so did her temperature. Her cheeks burned. She quaked, deep down.

"Good. It's not strictly necessary, but a bed is preferred under these circumstances."

He hadn't touched her, but she felt almost as if he had. This was much like her dream. Her heart pounded, her insides quivered, and she wanted…she wanted so much.

Too much, too fast. What would he think of her if she was too bold? She looked past him. "Would you like something to drink? Something to eat besides the stew? I have a very nice sweet bread, cheese, and a good red wine."

He ignored her offer. "Take off your dress."

Instantly, she wanted to do just that, even though it was too fast and shockingly inappropriate. "What about you?"

He smiled, and it was unlike his previous forced grin. She liked it. "I'm not wearing a dress."

"You know what I mean," she said, giving in to a smile of her own. If he was going to be so bold, why couldn't she? Why should she pretend that he was here for anything other than the bedding they both desired?

He took a step toward her; she backed toward the door to her bedroom. "You've seen a man unclothed?"

"Well, yes." Not like this, but living in The City amongst shifters, she'd seen naked men and women all her life.

His dark green eyes flashed. "Do you often invite strange men into your bed?"

Again, honesty was best. He would know soon enough, in any case. "No. You are the first." And the last? Could this fisherman be the husband she'd decided to take? Maybe. Maybe not. It was possible that if she just got this craving out of her system she could move on with her life as a single woman until she found a *proper* husband. She didn't know Kalum well, but already she knew proper was not a word which could be used to describe him. Perhaps after this joining with an ordinary man she'd no longer be tormented by dreams of what she'd never have. A true mate. Then again…

"You're thinking too much," she whispered.

"What?" Kalum asked as he took another step closer.

"Nothing," she said. "I'm talking to myself."

She opened the door to her bedroom and stepped inside. It was cooler here, the light dimmer. As soon as the sun set it would be dark, and she wanted to see Kalum naked before that happened. She wanted that very much.

Many human women were shy about their bodies,

but it was not the way of her people. Anwyn and Caradon alike were earthy, unreserved, and passionate. Rori began to unbutton the bodice of her dress, and Kalum unbuttoned his shirt. Beyond the window, distant waves crashed. She'd come to like the sound, perhaps even to need it.

"Your bed is very small," he said, glancing behind her.

"It will suffice."

"Yes, I suppose it will."

She undressed, and so did he. Their disrobing was methodical, unhurried, but with every second that passed her desire grew sharper. Keener. Rori tried to tell herself that this was simply something that needed to be done, like scratching an itch or sneezing when she inhaled a grain or two of pepper. But as she removed the last of her underthings she admitted that there was something more going on. To lie with a man was meaningful. To take a man into her bed for the first time meant something.

Suddenly she was glad it was him. She was glad it was Kalum who would share this moment with her, not Ben or any other man from this village or beyond.

There was no emotion on his face, no sign that he felt the rightness of the moment as she did. He attempted to appear unaffected but she saw, as he removed his trousers, that he was not. Physically, at least, he was very much affected.

Naked, anxious, they stood close. She could feel the heat from his body, smell his skin, feel the energy they created, an energy that made the air between them shimmer. The last light of day barely lit the room, but it was enough. They had not yet touched, he had not kissed her and she did not know if he would or not. Kissing was not strictly necessary, she supposed, but she wanted it.

"You're shaking," he said in a low voice. "Are you afraid?"

"No," she whispered.

"Good."

He did not kiss her. Instead he slipped his hand between her thighs and stroked with large, warm fingers. Rori gasped, at the pleasure, at the longing, at the sheer beauty of the moment. It was a dream come to life, a melding of two worlds.

The man who caressed her, the man she wanted so very badly, was the fisherman Kalum *and* he was her dream lover. He had come for her at last, and in the most unusual way. Her head fell back, her thighs parted to allow him greater access, and he took advantage of the move touching her harder, deeper. The world spun as knowledge washed through her, brain to toes.

"You're, you're…"

"Kalum. Your mate."

Chapter Four

Kalum laid Rori on the bed and followed her, holding her body close and looking deep into her eyes. Those eyes were hard; her body had tensed. She was furious with him. Perhaps she had a right to be angry. He'd been a dismal failure at wooing, and his fisherman ruse had not lasted very long at all. She had a million questions for which he could not possibly have adequate answers, and unless he was mistaken she wanted him to suffer.

But more than that, she wanted this. She wanted all he'd promised in a dream. He saw that truth in her eyes, too, felt it in the way she held her bare body against his.

"You followed me," she said.

"You ran away." His voice was not much more than a growl.

"You were late!"

"I was busy."

He touched her, spread her legs. She closed her eyes and her hips lifted toward him in invitation. "Stop talking," she commanded.

"As you command, princess."

"Don't call me…"

He kissed her then, placed his mouth on hers and gave in to the desire that had been all but consuming him. She wrapped her legs around him, moaned into his mouth and flicked her tongue in a way that drove him mad. This could be over for both of them in a matter of seconds, but that's not what he wanted and it was not what Rori needed.

He took his mouth from hers but he continued to

kiss her. Her throat, her breasts, the perfect skin of her torso. Sucking gently he reveled in her as he explored her fine, warm flesh with his lips and his tongue. He tasted her flesh but he also tasted the beating of her heart and the passion in her blood in a way he had not expected and could not explain. Even angry Rori was intoxicating and addictive.

She was perfection. She was his.

Her fingers threaded in his hair and she held on tight. Eyes closed, heart pounding, she gave in to her instincts, as he was giving into his.

"Do it," she ordered, throwing one leg over his hip. "Get this over with so I will know peace again."

"Is that what you think?" he asked. "Do you think lying with me is a chore that will bring you peace?"

"Heaven above, I hope so," she whispered.

He wanted to make this last, but he also wanted to see her as they joined. There was not much light left in the day; soon she would be lost in darkness. He wanted to take his time and make her beg, but she wasn't the only one following primal instincts. He wanted her as much, perhaps more, than she wanted him.

He pushed inside her body. Slow, as easy as was possible. It took all his patience and restraint to continue in such a way. She was tight, hot, wet, untouched and untrained. But her body understood what it wanted and needed. Instinctively, she knew what to do. Her hips rose to meet his easy thrust. Eyes closed, head thrown back, she wrapped both legs around him and pulled him in. Deeper, harder. And then she whispered, "Do not be gentle with me, Kalum."

With those words he forgot restraint and followed his own instincts. They joined completely at last, her body and his, each one driving toward culmination. Perhaps Rori was untested, but she was not shy and she did not hold back. She clutched at him and screamed, and then he felt her inner muscles convulsing around him as she found release. He came with her, giving over at last, after waiting so long…

Rori collapsed onto the bed, boneless, sated but still angry. After a few deep breaths, she pressed small delicate hands against his chest and pushed. It was an ineffectual motion, one he could easily ignore. But he did not. He rolled away to lie at her side.

"If you are truly my mate, and I have not yet fully accepted that you are, then you waited long enough to come to me," she said, an odd mixture of satisfaction and scorn in her voice.

"As I said, I was busy," he said easily.

Her eyes opened. Again he was struck by the color and power there. Her eyes were blue and gold, like no others. "Busy bedding women not your mate, I imagine, like any other heathen Caradon. Busy carousing before tying yourself down to your mate."

Kalum smiled. "You could not be more wrong, princess." He raked a finger across her cheek. "You are not the only one who was a virgin before this night."

Rori rolled away, grabbed a robe, and pulled it on. She wasn't shy, but she could still feel Kalum as if he remained inside her, and to stand before him naked made her feel much more vulnerable than she cared for.

"Do not call me princess," she commanded.

"Why?" He rose up on his elbow.

"I've left that life behind."

"I thought maybe it was because of the Ksana demon who uses that name. She's a nasty one. It would not do for someone to hear you called Princess and think you were her."

"I do not concern myself with the demons," she said,

lifting her chin.

He growled, a little. "You'll concern yourself when they show up on your doorstep."

She pulled the robe tighter. One of the demon daughters *had* just recently shown up on her doorstep. Not that she would share that information with Kalum, or anyone else. "Why is it that you know so much about the demons?"

His smile faded. "I told you. I've been busy."

Fighting the demons, she now understood. Fighting a war that was not his own. Her sisters had all been claimed by their mates before the age of twenty, while her mate had apparently preferred war to claiming her. Another reason for her to feel inadequate. As if she needed another.

Already she understood Kalum well enough to know that he could not find out about Lucia. If he'd been fighting the nastiest of the demons then he would kill poor Lucia without a second thought. He wouldn't stop to ask if she was truly evil; he wouldn't care that she hadn't asked to be fathered by a demon.

"You could have waited for me," he added in a lowered voice.

"*You* could have come to The City years ago."

He shook his head. "It was a hard thing for me to accept. I kept waiting for the urge to run to you to go away. I kept waiting for the dreams to stop."

Dreams. Her heart leapt, but she tried hard not to let her reaction show. "It's possible that you're not my mate. Our physical attraction could be entirely normal. Ordinary." Isn't that what she wanted more than anything? An ordinary life?

Again he shook his head. "I think not."

She knew how to make him leave her, but she didn't shift. She didn't want him to know, didn't want him to laugh at her the way her brothers had. More, she didn't want to see pity in his eyes. She was descended from the most powerful beings in all of Columbyana, and yet she had been cursed.

"Come back to bed," he said.

"Why?"

"Because we are not finished."

"I beg to differ." Her words were cold, but inside, inside she grew warm. She wanted him again. The last of the light faded as she stood there, torn, angry, wanting, as they were thrust into darkness.

"We have a lot of lost time to make up for," Kalum said, and there was so much promise and passion in his voice she took a step toward the bed. And another. She dropped her robe onto the floor and crawled onto the bed. She wanted his flesh pressed to hers again, wanted him inside her. That was where he belonged, for now.

She did her best to make her words sound detached. "Do not think I come to you because I care for you. Do not think there is love in this bed. You are necessary, and that is all."

Necessary. It was a good word for the hours that followed. They didn't talk much. There were no gentle kisses. Rori screamed when she found release. She even bit him a time or two. He could not get enough of her, and no wonder. They had a lot of lost time to make up for. He'd ignored what he'd known to be true for years, denying her and himself. When he held Rori in his arms he could not remember why he'd fought this for so long.

They made love until her scent was so deeply imbedded in his skin he did not think it would ever wash off. Not that he wanted to wash away the smell. His scent was now hers, too. It was a way of claiming her, he supposed, a way of marking her as his own. Now and forever. Even when they were far apart.

"I could live in you," he whispered as he spread her legs and entered her again, as the sun rose and light once again filled the room.

Rori responded to his touch in a way he'd never expected. Completely, with abandon. She didn't make love as he'd imagined a princess might. Then again, she was an *Anwyn* princess. Primitive, animalistic…and more beautiful than he'd imagined any woman could be.

He expected her to kick him out of the bed, now that the morning had arrived. After all, she'd made it very clear that all she wanted from him was sex. She did tell him— whispering, breathless—that it was time for him to go. She was too sated to insist with much fervor. Her request was half-hearted, at best. He sat up and swung his legs over the side of the bed, and she was instantly at his back. She clung to him, and he smiled.

Then her fingers traced the marking on his back. "Is this what I think it is?"

"A dragon, yes," he responded. "At least, that is what I have been told. I cannot see it without a couple of mirrors and I have never cared enough to go to the trouble."

"Whatever possessed you to get a dragon tattoo?"

"It's not a tattoo."

She kissed him there, then whispered. "What is is, then?"

Good question. He'd never been certain what to call it. "I was born with a large birthmark there. As I grew the skin stretched and changed, and gradually it took the shape you see now."

"What does it mean?" she whispered.

"I don't have any idea. Maybe it doesn't mean anything at all."

She sighed. Her hands drifted down his back and then away.

"There is a legend in this village. Have you noticed all

the dragons on the signs along the main road? The tavern, the inn, the town hall."

He'd seen the signs, but hadn't thought much about them. "What kind of legend?"

She lowered her voice, as one speaking of a prophecy might. One small, gentle hand rested against his side. "They say a dragon sleeps in a hidden cave on the bluffs above the sea, and when the village is in danger it will rise to save them."

Coincidence. "Dragons have not existed for a very long time. Any such creature sleeping in any cave died off long ago."

"Unless…it's you."

No, that was impossible. He did not intend to stay here. The war with the demon daughters was nowhere near won. His sword, and his claws, were still necessary. "It's just an odd birthmark, nothing more."

Rori hummed for a moment as she traced the mark on his shoulder with a single fingertip he felt as if it reached inside him. "Come back tonight," she whispered.

"I thought you said this was a…"

"Don't throw my words back at me," she interrupted. "I don't know what to make of this, what to make of you. I need time to think, so get some sleep and come back tonight." There it was again, that sigh that said too much. "I have something to show you."

Knowing that she would be lying with a man last night, Rori had taken precautions so she would not conceive a child. She'd expected Ben, not Kalum, and now she wondered…

No, nothing had changed. Kalum deserved to know the truth about her before he decided whether or not he wanted to stay. She had no intention of returning to the

Mountains of the North, that vast range that was home to her people and his. If he wanted her he would have to stay here. Would he agree to live in a place so far from home that shifting wouldn't come easily, or at all?

He had not changed last night, the third night of the full moon. At home, he would have changed as a matter of course. Here it was a chore. Did he miss it? Did he long to run as mountain cat?

As the day progressed, Rori began to accept what was obviously truth. The mate she'd thought not to exist had finally come for her. He was a Caradon, and he'd waited too long to find her. He'd run away from the mountains her people and his called home to fight a war which was not his own, instead of accepting what was meant to be and claiming her. But he did have a few fine attributes to go along with his obvious failings. He was strong and handsome, and he had waited for her as she had waited for him.

Her Anwyn mother and Caradon father had created five relatively normal shifter children, and her. What would she and Kalum create if they had children? She wasn't sure she wanted to know.

The day dragged on. She needed sleep, but patients came to her, as always. She was distracted, sore from head to toe, and confused about many things, but she did her best.

She thought of Lucia's particular problem, and in between visitors she pored through old books searching for a clue to a cure.

Perhaps she could find a cure for her own ailment, as well.

It was late afternoon when an agitated neighbor knocked on her door. Rori had treated Adith Farley for headaches and toothaches, but for the most part she was healthy and friendly. A good neighbor, if a bit of a busybody.

"Did you hear?" Adith wrung her hands as she walked into Rori's cottage.

"Hear what?"

"Ben, Ben Skrewd. He's dead."

Rori gasped as she thought of the healthy young man she'd spoken to just yesterday. "What happened? He seemed so well last time I saw him."

"It was not a natural death," Adith whispered.

The hair on the back of Rori's neck stood up and danced. She knew what was coming before Adith continued with a hoarsely whispered, "Someone killed him. His heart was ripped out of his chest."

Chapter Five

As he walked toward Rori's cottage, Kalum could feel eyes on him. Years of war and his Caradon instincts combined to put him on high alert. He continued on his path, not increasing his pace or slowing down, but he listened and glanced side to side without being obvious. Words drifted to him, softly spoken words human ears would not be able to hear.

That's him. He threatened Ben and a few hours later poor Ben is dead.

Ben said he threatened to use his bones as toothpicks. The poor fella was scared, and rightly so.

He's big. Can we take him?

Instead of continuing on his path, Kalum turned toward a small shop. He wouldn't take trouble to Rori's door. He needed to know what had happened, what he was being accused of. Ben, the man he'd intercepted just last evening, was apparently dead. He was innocent of any wrongdoing—well, of most wrongdoing—and he was certainly innocent of murder.

But he had threatened the murdered man, and he was a stranger here.

The small shop he found himself in sold tobacco, sweets, tea, and wine. It was a place to indulge in one's pleasures. Just this morning Rori had mentioned the town's dragon legend. Sure enough, a small red dragon adorned the sign behind the counter at the far end of the shop. Again he thought coincidence. Not that he'd ever put much stock in coincidence before.

Kalum wasn't sure yet what would happen with Rori,

but he'd shared her bed and would again, so perhaps he should take her a gift. Wasn't that expected when a man wooed a woman?

Besides, shopping would give him an excuse for spending a few moments here. Someone would confront him about what had happened to Ben or they would not. He'd prefer the confrontation to happen here or on the street, rather than in Rori's home.

He studied the offerings, and finally decided on either wine or tea. Perhaps both. He half listened for activity behind him as he perused the teas, which were arranged neatly near elaborate and plain teapots and cups. Sure enough, it wasn't long before three men entered the small store behind him. One cleared his throat. Kalum turned to face the men who filled the doorway.

One was elderly, another was portly, and the third was bone thin. He could take them all in a matter of moments, if it came to that, but for now he held back. Until he knew their intentions, it would be best to wait. He had not come here looking for trouble.

"I'm constable of this village," the thin one said. "I have some questions for you."

Kalum leaned against the counter, trying for a nonchalant pose even though he was anything but relaxed. "Of course. How can I assist you?"

"Where were you last night?"

Kalum hesitated. When he was done here he might very well be leaving Rori behind. If she refused to come with him, if she did not want the only life he could offer her, he could and would leave her. He was a soldier, but he had not yet spoken to Rori about what it meant to be a soldier's wife. That was the only life he had to offer.

No matter what happened, whether Rori left this place with him or stayed here alone, he did not want to sully her reputation. "Why do you ask?"

"Ben Skrewd was killed last night."

"I'm sorry to hear that," Kalum said honestly. Not that he would miss old Ben, but apparently the fellow's death was going to cause him a lot of trouble.

"I hear the two of you had a confrontation yesterday."

Kalum smiled. "It was more of a conversation than a confrontation."

"That's not how he told it," the old man muttered.

Kalum turned his eyes to the old man. "I didn't kill him, if that's what you're asking."

"So, where were you last night?" the constable asked again.

Kalum took a deep breath and tried to find the words to make this right without involving Rori, but it was a soft, familiar voice who answered.

"He was with me."

The men turned and parted, allowing Rori to enter the shop. Gods, she was beautiful. Had she chosen the pretty blue dress with him in mind? It showed a bit more skin than the others he'd seen her wear, and the color was so much like her eyes…and he was a fool for noticing either.

"It looks as though Ben was killed very late last night," the constable said. "He could have done to deed after he left you."

Rori didn't hesitate. "He did not leave until the sun had risen."

The old man's eyebrows rose. The fat man looked at the floor and blushed. The constable remained calm. "Now, Rori, you wouldn't lie to me to protect this man, would you?"

"No, I would not." Her eyes met his, strong as ever. "Kalum is far from perfect, and I have no doubt that he is capable of murder in the right circumstances. As we all are. But he did not kill Ben."

"I don't need you to defend me," Kalum said.

"Apparently you do," she argued sharply.

Rori was a part of this community, and the constable believed her. For now, at least. But he nodded in Kalum's direction. "Until this is sorted out, I expect you to stay close. You don't plan on going anywhere soon, do you?"

"I have not yet decided how long I will remain in your village."

"Don't leave until I give you permission to do so."

Kalum opened his mouth to argue, but Rori spoke before he could say a word. "He's not leaving. Not yet."

Her life had been so simple before Kalum had entered it. First in her dreams, then as a beachside distraction, then as a lover. As the mate she had thought never to know.

And now this. No matter what happened with the two of them, if he stayed or if he left, in the eyes of the village they were connected. By murder and seduction, they would forever be linked.

There were other villages, other places she could hide, but she liked it here. This place was becoming home. Why should she have to leave?

Back in her cottage, she and Kalum did not talk about what had happened to poor Ben. She knew he was innocent, knew precisely where he'd been all night. What she did not know was if the murder was somehow connected to her invitation or Kalum's warning. Had they put Ben in danger simply by bringing him into their orbit? It seemed unlikely, but she could not be sure of anything.

As soon as darkness fell, Rori took Kalum's hand and led him around the cottage and toward the beach. An almost full moon lit the sky, and she noted that he looked at that moon longingly. He was too far from home and the full phase was past. The pull was not gone, but was also not what it should be.

This village was beginning to feel like home to her. Could it ever be home for a Caradon? Would Kalum ever be himself here?

On the sand, she released his hand and turned to look at him. "You deserve to know why I left home, why I was so certain I had no mate and never would. Before this thing between us goes too far, you have to know."

"There's nothing you can say…"

And with those words, she shifted.

One moment Rori was standing before him, reddish brown hair caught in a gentle breeze, blue dress simple and a little loose on her fine frame. Then before his eyes a flock of small birds burst into the air where she'd once stood, and her dress lay empty on the sand. There was no time at all between woman and birds, no awkward moment where she was caught in the middle of a shift.

The birds flew around him, circling, chirping, moving the wind. Moonlight lit them—her—and he realized these were not just any birds.

Bluebirds, with feathers the color of Rori's eyes and breasts the color of her hair, flitted around him. They were small, and fast, and so many he could not begin to count them. He had never seen anything more beautiful.

He laughed, amazed by what he was seeing. She didn't like that. He knew she was displeased by his laughter because one small bird pecked at his head. Just once. He offered a hand and one of the birds lit there. Another on his shoulder. Another on his forearm.

Kalum had never even heard of such a wonder; and it was not even a night of the full moon! He'd heard tales of her mother and grandmother, knew that some said they could shift without the pull of the moon, but to see it happen before his eyes was wondrous.

The birds that had lit on him took flight at once to join the others. And then they swirled around one spot for a split second and Rori was there again. Naked now, hair wild, blue eyes shining.

"By the heavens," he whispered. "You…"

"Don't say it," she said, grabbing her dress from the sand and holding it before her body. In the moonlight he could see the tears in her eyes. "It's embarrassing. I come from a family of powerful creatures, and I…I'm a flock of damned bluebirds."

He took her shoulders and held in her place, though she looked poised to run. He made her look at him as he said, in a voice touched with awe, "You are an amazing creature."

"Don't make fun of me," she whispered.

"I'm not. Rori, love, you can fly."

Chapter Six

She didn't know what most surprised her. That Kalum seemed to be truly impressed or that he had called her *love*.

"It's unnatural," she whispered. "How can you see anything more than that?"

He lifted her into his arms and carried her around the cottage and through the red door. He kicked the door shut behind him and placed her on her feet. She was still naked, had her dress clutched in her hand. Tangled hair fell across her face.

For the first time in a very long time, she didn't feel like a freak. *You can fly.* Even more important, for the first time since she'd shifted and discovered what she was, she didn't feel alone. Kalum knew her secret, and he didn't hate her for it. He didn't feel sorry for her. He *had* laughed, briefly, but that laughter had been touched with surprise, not derision.

He called her *love*.

He'd put her down but he continued to hold her gently, as if she might break. She felt treasured and wanted and loved. If only she had found him sooner. If only she had known he existed. She would have scoured the world for him, if she'd known. She let the dress she clutched fall to the floor between them.

"Where were you?" She placed her head on his chest and leaned in. "All these years, I waited. I thought I had no mate, I thought no one would ever…" *love me.* She was not ready to say those words out loud. "I thought no man would ever be mine." She tilted her head back and looked up. "Why didn't you come?"

He brushed her hair away from her face. She knew she was a mess; she always was after she shifted. He didn't seem to mind. "I tried to deny you. I am Caradon. We do not mate for life, we are not haunted by one woman who is meant for us. We do not dream of a woman so real and wondrous that no other can take her place."

He'd mentioned dreams before, and she wondered if they had been as real, as frustrating, as hers had been. "You dreamed of me often?"

"Every night."

Just yesterday she'd been determined to lie with Kalum and then let him go. One night to end the pain, one bedding to ease her frustration so she could move on with her so-called normal life. That was before she'd realized who he was. That was before her life had changed, before she felt...like this. "Lie with me."

"Gladly." He took a step toward the bedroom.

"Never leave me."

"I could not, even if I wished to."

"Do you wish to?" She unfastened his trousers and slipped her hand inside.

"No."

"Kiss me."

"Your wish is my command, princess."

She forgot about poor Ben, as Kalum claimed her again and again. All through the night, he loved her. They slept but never for very long. She woke wanting him and he was there. Without him she was empty. Alone. Sad.

The sun was high in the sky and she was fast asleep when someone began banging on her door. Rori leapt from the bed, grabbed a wrapper, and ran to answer. Just because she had discovered love—if that's what this was—that didn't mean her patients would cease to become ill. Some of them would be shocked and dismayed to find Kalum here, if he left the bedroom and showed himself, but as shocking as it was, she didn't care. He was a part of her life, for now, and his presence didn't affect her ability to heal.

She was surprised to see the demon—half demon, demon's daughter—before her. Lucia looked different today. Stronger, perhaps. Less uncertain. She certainly no longer appeared to be shy.

Rori stepped away from the door. "Come in."

She hadn't had much time to do the research she'd promised. Kalum had proved a definite distraction. "I'm afraid I have no answers for you just yet."

"Too busy spreading your legs for the cat to help me, I suppose," Lucia snapped as she slammed the door behind her.

Rori took a step back, alarmed by Lucia's tone and by her knowledge. "There is no need to be vulgar."

"Is there not?" Lucia conveyed such a sad mixture of emotions. She was angry and sad, desperate and powerful. "You said three days and it has been three days. I tried to wait, I swear I did. Time is running out for me. The demon screams in my ear. An evil man, a wizard, he whispers to me as well and I cannot make him stop. I cannot make either of them *stop*." She cocked her head. "He wants me to kill your cat. He wants me to eat his heart the way I…" Lucia choked on the end of the sentence.

"The way you what?" Rori asked, but she knew. In an instant, she *knew*.

Tears shone in Lucia's eyes, but none fell. "I could not help myself. The moon was full and I was hungry. The farmer's heart fed me well, but soon I will need another."

Rori didn't hear the bedroom door open, didn't hear Kalum's step, but she noticed how Lucia's eyes shifted in that direction and went wide. Rori turned a bit and glanced back. Kalum stood there, bare-chested and bare-footed, wearing only his trousers. He looked intimidating, even to her, but could a demon be intimidated by a man?

Half demon, she reminded herself. Lucia was as much human as she was demon, as much good as she was evil. Ben's heart aside. Did that matter?

"You." Lucia whispered. "Damned cat. They hate you, so much. You killed many of my sisters. You would kill me, given the chance."

"Rori, who is this?" Kalum asked. He never took his eyes from Lucia.

Lucia turned her attention to Rori. "No one can kill him but you," she whispered. "No one can kill me but..." She stopped, seemed to choke, then continued on. "To-night, on the beach to the north. If you do not come I will burn this village and every living thing in it to ash." And with that Lucia was gone. In a puff of smoke that momentarily blinded Rori, the daughter of the Isen demon simply disappeared.

"A demon is here?" Kalum shouted. "And you *know* her?"

"She came to me looking for help," Rori explained calmly.

He shouted, "There is no help for the likes of her. She ate Ben Skrewd's heart!"

Rori looked almost contrite, as if she'd been the one to kill the poor farmer. "I don't think she could help herself."

"Oh, well, that makes it all right, then."

He should not be angry with Rori. She didn't have his experience with the half demons, she didn't know how rarely they could be saved.

"She wants me to fix her, and I told her I would try to find a way." Rori looked at the floor. "I think it's too late, now. Ben…"

He was there, before her, holding her against her pain. "I'm sorry. I should not have yelled at you."

"You didn't yell," she said against his chest. "Much."

For a few minutes they just stood there. He'd never felt quite like this, but then he'd never had a lover before. Maybe it was just the act of sex that made him feel this way. As if Rori belonged here, in his arms. As if he would never leave her.

Nonsense.

"I'll go to the constable and offer my assistance in bringing the demon in."

"Lucia," Rori whispered.

"What?"

"Her name is Lucia."

It was best not to know their names, he'd learned. It was easier to kill them if you dismissed their human halves and concentrated only on the demon in them. Yes, some had been saved. Thanks to a powerful healing witch, some had been separated from the demon who spoke to them in dreams and in their moments of weakness. But that separation was rare. And none of those who had been saved had taken to eating human hearts, as Lucia had.

Kalum was a soldier, not a wizard or an emperor. He fought, he killed, he protected. He had no special powers beyond his ability to shift; he did not see the future or read minds.

And yet he knew without doubt that Lucia could not be saved.

Chapter Seven

Kalum did his best to convince Rori to stay behind while he disposed of the demon Lucia, but she was stubborn.

"I am meant to be there," she argued in a maddeningly calm voice.

He shouldn't care so much. He'd known her for a few days, if he discounted the dreams, and he'd planned all along to leave her behind. Those plans had been easy, when he hadn't felt this way. And like it or not, he could not discount the dreams that had brought him to this place.

Rori was his. He'd grudgingly accepted that fact a long time ago, but he'd never felt it to his bones until now. She placed her hand on his face and she smiled at him, and he knew he would die to protect her.

The party that headed out of town just before sunset was small. Rori and Kalum; the constable and one deputy; the singer from the town's tavern, a young man who had volunteered because he was curious, and because he thought a great song might come out of the adventure. Dangerous thing, curiosity. But the singer carried a sword and seemed to know how to use it, so he might come in handy before the night was done.

One half demon alone should not be hard to kill, but Kalum had learned not to discount the unexpected. What if she was not alone? What if she had powers of which they knew nothing?

While the moon was bright it was no longer full, so Kalum would not have his feline form as a weapon. He'd face the demon as a man, as he'd done many times in the past.

Lucia hadn't bothered to hide; he wouldn't have to worry about a sneak attack out of the darkness. North of the village, on the sand near a craggy stone bluff, she'd built a bonfire that lit the skies as night fell. It was a beacon, calling them to her. Could it be a trap? Possibly. Perhaps she was simply overconfident. She would not be the first.

"I could not help her," Rori said. Her soft words barely reached him over the pounding waves and the wind touched with the scent of the sea. "I wanted to, I did, but there was no time to find a…a cure."

"There is one witch who can separate the woman from the demon, if the human half is very strong and willing to fight."

"Why didn't you tell me!" she snapped, running in the sand to draw closer, to match his longer stride. "We might have found a way to help Lucia."

Kalum shook his head. "Once she killed Ben, there was no longer a chance to save her. Trust me, I've seen this sort of thing before."

She was silent for a moment. "There are many of them? Many like Lucia?"

"Yes."

"How many?"

"No one really knows." He didn't point out to her that there were fewer of the demon's daughters since he'd joined the emperor's fight against them.

"They're just girls," Rori said. "They didn't ask to be sired by the Isen Demon."

"No, I suppose not. But I did not ask for my lot and you did not ask for yours. We are as we are, Rori, for better or for worse. So are they all."

She was quiet for a while. The bonfire that called to them seemed to grow no closer, for a while. And then it did. He could see the woman, the demon, standing before the fire. She waited for them, backlit by the flames, the ocean breeze whipping her skirt and her hair around her. Either the wind on that part of the beach was fiercer than it was elsewhere, or the demon created her own whirl-wind.

The three men who accompanied him and Rori slowed their pace, instinctively falling back. Soon he saw Lucia's face, he felt the heat of the fire. It did not soothe him at all to note that the demon's face was streaked with tears.

She looked not at him but at Rori. "Have you come to save me or to kill me?"

"Lucia," Rori began. "Let us…"

"You cannot help me, can you? I am beyond saving."

"No one is beyond saving," Rori argued.

Kalum knew that was a lie, but he didn't say so aloud. That was the kind of thing one had to learn for oneself, and he did not want to see Rori jaded just yet. That time would eventually come for her.

Lucia lifted her hand and waved it, and Kalum felt as if he'd been kicked in the chest by a mule. He landed in the sand, hard, and heard the surprised grunts of the other men. Rori was not affected. She alone stood toe to toe with the demon's daughter.

And he could not move. No matter how much he wished it, he could not help her.

"Kill me," Lucia whispered. "Or I will burn the vil-lage and everyone in it, as I warned you I would. It's me or all of them. You choose, Rori. Only you."

"I can't." No matter what Kalum said, there had to be a way to save the poor girl.

"I don't want to lose my head. The only other way

for me to die is by fire." Lucia glanced back at the bonfire that blazed behind her. "I can't do it myself. He won't let me."

He. The demon that whispered to all his daughters or the wizard Lucia had said spoke to her as well? Rori tried to imagine having evil voices that were not her own in her head, and she could not. Such a thing would drive anyone mad.

"I don't know what to do, Lucia. I can't save you and I can't kill you."

"You *can* kill me!" Lucia snapped. "You have fire, like your father."

Rori shook her head. Lucia had said that before, but Rori knew she had no fire. She possessed no abilities that would help in this situation. What could bluebirds do? Nothing. Nothing at all. "You're wrong." Maybe Kalum, who had that tattoo or birthmark or whatever it was on his shoulder. Maybe he…

"I'll prove it to you," Lucia said.

Four men, one of them Kalum, lay on the sand stunned. Lucia snapped a hand in their direction and the constable's deputy rose from the ground in an unnatural way. He was not in control of his body; he dangled as if suspended by invisible ropes. He screamed as his feet left the sand and he floated in the air.

Lucia lifted her other hand and thrust it in the floating man's direction. The deputy's chest opened and his heart flew into her hand. She looked at the heart for a moment then took a big bite that smeared her lips and her teeth with blood. She swallowed, then tossed the deputy's body and his torn heart into the fire.

Lucia smiled. Her mouth and her teeth were stained a sickening red. A drop of blood dribbled down her chin. She licked that drop away with a long, undulating tongue.

Rori was shocked into stillness and silence. She could not speak, she could not move. Until Lucia pointed to Kalum and his body began to rise...

Chapter Eight

Kalum had no control over his body; he was numb all over. For the first time in his life, he was unable to fight. His sword had dropped to the ground as he'd risen and lay several feet below. Even if he could move, he would not be able to reach it. The demon would do to him what she'd done to the poor deputy, unless Rori killed her first.

Rori was not a killer.

He dangled in the air, waiting for the pain in his chest, knowing this was his last moment on the earth. He'd always known his life might end in such a way, but he'd had no idea that it would come so soon after finding what he'd never known existed for him. Love.

With effort, he twisted his head so he could see Rori. She was terrified and angry and lost. She healed people, she didn't kill. She did not have the spirit of a warrior; she was gentle; she was kind. Judging by the stunned expression on her face, if she did find herself capable of taking a life it would come too late.

It was a struggle, but he tried to say the words. "I love you." He didn't know if the words would reach Rori over the wind and the roar of the fire, but he wanted her to know. He needed to say the words before he was taken so violently from this life. And then there it was, a sharp pain in his chest, a sensation of tugging and tearing.

Without warning, Rori burst into a flock of bluebirds.

The tugging in his chest instantly ceased. Lucia was surprised by Rori's transformation, and it shocked her enough to make her stop grabbing at his heart. She did not lose control entirely; Kalum still hung in the air, unable to move.

And then he was shocked, as well. The bluebirds swirled closely together, and in another burst they became a smaller number of larger blackbirds. Large, sharp beaks pecked at Lucia, who instinctively tried to protect herself by throwing her arms over her head. She screamed and Kalum dropped to the ground, landing hard in the sand.

For a moment he couldn't breathe, but he caught his breath and reached for his sword. His fingers closed around the hilt. He heard the other two men land on the sand behind him, with a thud and a grunt.

The blackbirds came together as the bluebirds had, flying as one in a dark mass. They swirled near the flames of Lucia's bonfire, apparently unafraid of the fire. Suddenly colors appeared where there had once been only silky black feathers. Green and gold and brown. And red.

He'd never seen a dragon before, did not believe them to exist, but where bluebirds and blackbirds had once been, what could only be a dragon now hovered in the air. Translucent wings flapped slowly; blazing red eyes set in a craggy bird-like face cut this way and that. A long red tail, large enough and powerful enough to smash a dozen men in one blow, swished through the air, creating its own wind. The dragon gained control of that tail and the massive wings and soared in the air for a moment, up to the bluff and back down again. The wind created by the flapping of large, veined wings made the bonfire flicker and the sand swirl.

The constable swore and the singer sobbed. Lucia, dress flapping violently around her, looked up, spread her arms, and smiled.

The dragon flew toward the ocean, turned, and circled back again. It—she—flew toward the bonfire and the demon, and in an instant Kalum realized what was about to happen. He scrambled to his feet. "Move!" he shouted, grabbing the constable's arm and pulling him along when the older man hesitated. The singer did not hesitate at all, but stood and ran, quick as he could in the soft sand, back toward home.

Lucia tossed her head back closed her eyes. Wind from the ocean and the dragon's flight pressed her dress to her body and sent her dark hair flowing back.

A stream of red hot fire left the dragon's mouth and consumed her. Kalum was almost certain he heard a softly whispered "thank you" before the demon turned to dust.

The dragon landed in the sand, on legs so thin they should not be able to support the weight of the body and wings. After one wobbly, uncertain moment, the legs steadied. The dragon's head turned and those red eyes landed on Kalum and the constable. How aware was Rori? Was she in control or was the dragon now the one in charge? With a dragon's instincts and appetites, there was no way to know what she might do next.

"Run," Kalum whispered to the constable, who did not hesitate to obey. And then Kalum took a step toward the dragon.

He'd called her an amazing creature when he'd thought she could shift into a flock of bluebirds when there was no full moon. To shift into ravens and a dragon…she was like no other.

Rori was the dragon of legend in this village. She was the reason for the birthmark that had been a mystery to him, and to others, all his life.

"I love you," he said, for the second time tonight.

The transformation was not as quick and easy as it had been when she'd shifted from bluebirds to woman. Again, colors swirled. Wings shrunk and feathers shimmered in the firelight. She screamed once, mid-shift, but it was a scream of fury, not of pain. Finally Rori stood before him, naked and afraid.

She collapsed onto the sand and he ran to her. Tears

streamed down her face, and she shook as if the night were cold. She was his Rori again, frail and soft and small. No, he could never think of her as frail again. She was stronger, more powerful, than anyone he had ever known. He lifted her, cradled her close. Rori took a deep breath and then she whispered in his ear.

"I love you, too."

Her dress was partially burned, so he left it on the sand near what was left of the demon. The deputy deserved a decent burial, but his body could not be retrieved until the bonfire had died down. There would be nothing left but bones and ashes.

Kalum began the long walk toward home, intending not to let Rori go until they reached her cottage. She didn't speak for a long while, not until the dying bonfire was not much more than a speck in the night behind them.

"I had no idea I could…I didn't know…"

"You were angry," he said.

"She was going to kill you," Rori whispered. "She was going to eat your heart. I could not allow that to happen." She glanced up at him. "Your heart belongs to me."

"Yes, it does."

Chapter Nine

Traditional marriage was not always the way of her people or Kalum's, but they were not living among those people. Marriage was the convention here, and when her children came—and they would come—she wanted them to be accepted, not scorned.

The constable and the singer—who'd gotten not one song but three out of his adventure, thus far—had told everyone what they'd seen, and for the past three days those she passed had stared at her in awe. A few had dropped to their knees as if she were a queen to be worshipped. She had not seen a single patient, though she did think that would change, in time.

She had other concerns, at this moment.

Her sisters had so far only given birth to males with the golden eyes of the Anwyn, and the same might be true of her. Then again, it might not be true. Kalum was Caradon and she was different. So far from the mountains their people called home her children might not shift at all. Then again…

It would be years before she knew with any certainty, so she wouldn't worry about that now. If their children were like her, well, she and Kalum would deal with that when the time came. They'd have years before they had to address that concern.

Dragon. Not really, she now knew in an instinctive way. In one of his songs the singer who'd witness her transformation called her Firebird, and that seemed more right to her than dragon. She was a Firebird, and there was no other like her in all the world. She wondered if she could summon the creature again. It was frightening, to control so much power. But she remembered what it had been like to become that beast, to own the skies, to possess and control both flight and fire.

At least she no longer thought herself weak…

She was the dragon—the Firebird—which graced so many signs in this village. She was the legendary creature destined to protect them all. From what? From others like Lucia? Had she already fulfilled her destiny by killing that one demon, or were others on their way?

That was a concern for another time. Today she was a bride, with a bride's worries. *Is my hair perfect? Is this dress pretty? Will my husband always love me?*

She wore a plain cream colored dress with a little fine lace around the bodice and she carried a bouquet of red roses which had been gathered from the vine at her cottage. Kalum was dressed nicely, too. The priest was happy to marry them, and there was a decent crowd present in the chapel. Her patients; the constable; shopkeepers and housewives and farmers. Some of them were her neighbors and friends, while others were simply curious. She didn't care why they came. They were all witnesses to the start of her new life.

The ceremony was barely underway when the doors to the chapel opened. Not slowly and not quietly, but with a loud whoosh and a bang.

Rori turned her head, curious. She could almost feel herself pale when she saw who was standing there.

"Who are they?" Kalum asked.

Rori took a deep breath before answering. "My family."

As the newcomers approached, Rori gave a quick account of who was who. Queen Mother Juliet was in the lead. She didn't look like any grandmother Kalum had ever seen, in fact appeared to be far too young and much too attractive to be anyone's granny. When he expressed his surprise Rori explained that her grandmother was special in many ways, and he accepted that as true. Her grandfather Ryn didn't look much like the grandfather of a fully grown woman, either. Nor did he look like a man anyone with a lick of sense would want on the opposing side of a fight, whether that fight was all-out war or a family squabble.

"I told you we would arrive on time," Juliet said to her daughter Keelia, the current Queen of the Anwyn, as they neared the altar. The King was present, too, along with two sisters, their husbands, and a half dozen royal guards. None of them looked happy.

"Barely," Ryn replied in a voice that rumbled.

Juliet continued in a sweet voice. "Rori never would've discovered her true ability under the restrictions she's lived with all her life. She had to be on her own, whether you liked the idea or not."

Ryn sighed. No, it was more of a growl. "Another damned Caradon."

Those guests in attendance watched, some wide-eyed and leaning forward to get a better view, others slinking down in their seats so as not to call attention to themselves.

"He loves her. Nothing else matters." The matriarch of Rori's clan looked at Kalum with those striking gold eyes, and it was there that he saw her age. Her eyes were wise, a little tired. They were the eyes of a woman who has known sadness and joy and adventure. "And he will be father to remarkable children, so stop glaring at him. Kalum is family now."

Family was foreign to most Caradon. Close knit families were all but unheard of among his people. Rori's kin filled the aisle of the small chapel.

They were an impressive lot, he had to admit. Large, handsome, scantily dressed. And some of them were furious. With him. The priest and the onlookers had been stunned into silence. Stunned or scared. Both, most likely.

It was Kalum who stepped toward the newcomers and indicated the seats that remained available in the back of the chapel. "If you don't mind, I would like to proceed with the wedding."

The Queen, who apparently didn't take well to orders or even suggestions directed her way, bristled, but the Queen Mother nodded and smiled. When it came to this particular family, she was the one in charge.

They sat, the ceremony proceeded, and for a few minutes Kalum could almost forget that at least two psychics, one fire-starter, and an impressive number of shape-shifters were seated in the back of the chapel. He could feel the animosity rolling off the men—and the Queen—in that group.

He suspected only Queen Mother Juliet kept them from stopping the ceremony. Perhaps he had one ally in the bunch. The most important one, lucky for him.

After the priest pronounced them man and wife Kalum kissed his bride, more briefly than he liked. She smiled, leaned into him and whispered, "They will try to make me go home, but I want to stay here, at least for now. The village needs us, or soon will, and I like the sea."

It had always been his plan to leave this place behind. It had been his plan to walk away from Rori if she did not wish to come with him. But now he knew his place was here, with her. In time the war would come to them. Until then…

"I suspect they won't take your refusal to return to The City with anything resembling grace."

"They will not."

He glanced to the side and saw Queen Keelia, stalking down the aisle. They only had seconds before a confrontation.

"Whatever you want, wife."

"I want you."

"You have me."

Rori took his arm and turned to face her mother with a wide smile on her face. It was that smile that made Queen Keelia stop in her tracks well before the altar. A range of emotions crossed her face. Confusion, annoyance, and—quickly—a reluctant acceptance. And Kalum realized that the loving mother, Queen to a powerful race of beings and his mother-in-law, had never seen her daughter so happy.

"Mother," Rori said, her spine straight and her voice clear as a bell. "I have fire…"

* * * * * * * * *

Read on for an excerpt from
Bride By Midnight

Bride by Midnight

Lyssa sighed in relief when her groom arrived, a little late but in one piece, and not appearing to be ill or injured. Kyran was well-dressed, his long dark blond hair was nicely styled, but he looked...not at all happy. She wondered what had delayed him. She'd been so worried that assisting her father with the delivery to Empress Morgana would make her late, but still she'd had to wait for Kyran. Did he not realize how anxious she would become when he didn't arrive on time? He knew of her sad past where weddings were concerned, so he should realize how his tardiness would worry her. It was a terrible way to start their new life together.

The room was dismally and sparsely occupied. Her

father and stepmother, the holy man who would perform the ceremony, an anxious bride, and a nervous groom who'd arrived alone, without a single family member or friend as his guest. Lyssa was suddenly aware that there was not one cheerful face in the room. Sinmora attempted a smile, but it wasn't genuine and didn't last long. Should both bride and groom be miserable on their wedding day? It didn't seem right, but neither did a lifetime alone. So what was she to do? If the witch's prophecy had been correct, if her dreams of an achingly lonely darkness were more than simple nightmares, then Kyran was her last chance for all that she desired. A family. A home of her own. He was her *last chance* to become a wife before she turned twenty-three. Maybe they would learn to love one another, in time. At the very least, she hoped they would become friends.

She was a little surprised that not one member of Kyran's family had come with him. Was this not a happy occasion, for him to take a wife? Maybe they were angry because he intended to leave the farm. It had already been decided that he would live here and would immediately go to work for her father. Maybe his family knew of her unfortunate past and they were worried for him. Maybe they liked her even less than Kyran did.

Truly, there was nothing she could say about the groom's lack of a wedding party, since none of her own friends had come to the house for this ceremony. They all had very good reasons why they couldn't make it; they were busy with their own husbands and children and responsibilities. But she did wonder if perhaps they simply could not bear the drama of yet another disastrous almost-wedding.

Lyssa lifted her chin, dismissing all her worries as best she could and concentrating on the positive. She *would* be married before she turned twenty-three. Barely, as the sun was about to set on the last day of her twenty-second year, but it was as good as done. Kyran was here, having avoided death and disease on the way to their simple altar, and she was determined to see this done, in spite of her reservations.

Kyran walked over to her and took both her hands in his own. The way he looked into her eyes, the sorrow there...

Oh, no.

"I'm so sorry, Lyssa. I can't do this."

The floor beneath her feet started to spin, much as it had in the morning's nightmare. Her vision narrowed until all she could see was his traitorous, ordinary, not-very-bright face.

"Of course you can," she said, her heart pounding. She could feel it slamming against her chest so hard that surely everyone in the room heard her heartbeat. Her father took a step toward her. The priest sighed and dropped his gaze to the floor. Lyssa stopped her father's approach with a glance and a shake of her head and then she gave Kyran her attention. "If it makes you feel any better, I don't love you, either. There's more than love to marriage. We can make it work. We'll be friends, *partners*. We don't need love."

"I'm in love with someone else," Kyran whispered. "I thought I could do this. I was ready to marry you even though I knew it wasn't right for either of us. I thought it would be enough, to have you beside me as a friend and wife while I worked in your father's shop. Many people live worse lives. But then I met her, and I realized what true love could be."

Patience fading quickly, she snatched her hands from his. "You're leaving me for another woman?"

"Yes." Kyran smiled weakly. "I met her quite by accident, on the road through the woods just last week. Oh, Lyssa, she's so beautiful, so kind, and...I loved her at first glance, and she loves me."

She took a step back, the truth making her feel faint. "I truly do not need to hear this."

Kyran nodded, as if he understood. "We're leaving Arthes immediately. She has family in the Northern Province. Trust me, it's better this way. It would have ended badly for us. You deserve to find a love of your own, to feel what I now feel. Forgive me." With that he bowed curtly and exited the house as if a wolf were on his tail.

Lyssa stared at the door for a long while. Well, it seemed like a long while, as the seconds dragged on. Her parents and Father Kiril remained silent and still, disapprovingly solemn. She had done nothing wrong. She had given them no reason to be displeased with her, but...

Again she felt as if the floor were dropping out from under her, just as it had in her nightmare. The witch had been right. This was the end of her life. She would never marry, never give birth to a child, never have a home of her own. No man would ever love her. She would have no partner in life.

She wished with all her heart that she could convince herself the witch had been wrong all those years ago, but after four failed attempts at becoming a wife, what was she to think? The constant dreams of being alone in a dark room, where no one could see or hear or touch her...they were not only nightmares that woke her with a scream, they were horrifying predictions of her bleak future.

If there truly was a battle between darkness and light going on all around her, the darkness had won. Somehow it was her fault. There must be a weakness in her, something bad that she could not control...

It was Sinmora who broke the silence. "Oh, honey, I'm so sorry." Her hug was warm and genuine, and Lyssa allowed herself to wallow in it for a long moment. "There will be other men. Kyran was likely correct when he said a marriage between you two would go badly. It's a flighty man who meets a woman on the road and instantly thinks himself in love." She pursed her lips in disapproval. "You deserve better, dear. You will find happiness...one day."

Lyssa stepped away from the offered comfort. She steeled her spine, and forced her voice to remain steady and certain. "No, Vellance was right. This was my last chance. I'm going to live at home for the rest of my days." That might be unavoidable, but she didn't have to give in to whatever darkness might attempt to claim her. Besides, the magical part of the prediction could be completely wrong, an attempt by the witch to frighten her. As she had done all those years ago, Lyssa tried to convince herself that she could pick and choose which predictions she would accept and which ones she could dismiss as impossible. Her life would be what she made it, not a pre-ordained nightmare.

She desperately wanted to believe that to be true, even though she was no longer a child who was capable of convincing herself that she could pick apart a prediction and take from it only the tidbits that pleased her.

"I'll work with Papa," she said, swallowing her fear. "I'm good with numbers, and I'm good with people, too. Maybe it's too late for me, maybe I won't have a family of my own, but that doesn't mean I can't make a good life for myself." Her voice almost broke on that last sentence, but she wanted to believe it was true. Who needed a husband? And children were often disappointments to their mothers. Besides, it wasn't as if she looked forward to childbirth. Who would?

"Oh, that ridiculous prediction," Sinmora snapped. "That was nothing more than a crazy old woman's ramblings, and I can't believe you've taken it seriously all these years. You *will* marry. You *will* have a family." She reached out to caress Lyssa's hair. "You *will* know love."

Lyssa wished she could believe that.

The priest left the house without ever looking the

"bride" in the eye. Lyssa refused Sinmora's offers of a bite of supper, gave her father—who'd been silent and obviously disappointed through it all—a hug, and went to bed early. The narrow bed where she'd slept as a child would be her bed for life now, unless she decided to take vows at a nunnery. She shuddered at the thought. Not that the Sisters of Orianan weren't fine women who had dedicated their lives to doing good, but it was not Lyssa's dream to cut her hair and dress forever in black, and go months at a time without speaking a word aloud. Vow of silence? Horrors. Sacrifice was not in her nature. Neither was silence.

No, her father needed her. She was his only child, and she would do her duty and assist him in his trade. As there was no son to whom he could leave his assets, no son by marriage to assist him in his business, she would become like a son to him. Perhaps that was unconventional, but if it was that or a nunnery, her choice was an easy one.

There were worse ways to live her life, she supposed.

Eventually she fell into a deep sleep in the small bed she'd expected to share with a husband on this night, where the dreams of loneliness and darkness were more severe than ever before. The room where she found herself was so dark she couldn't see her own hand in front of her face, and when she began to fall, as she always did, she did not scream. Instead she accepted. She accepted the loneliness, the darkness…the disappointment. Why had she fought it all these years? Fear tried to rise within her, but she pushed it down; she fought it off and focused on the truth. This was her life now.

Briefly, something glimmered silver in the darkness. A knife. No, a sword, long and sharp and deadly. It teased her, made her believe that she was not alone after all. She should have been afraid of the blade, but…it would never hurt her. She knew that as one could know things in a dream. And then it was gone. Lyssa spread her arms and held her breath as she fell, and woke to the silent darkness of her lonely bed chamber, her body lurching a bit as if she actually had fallen from above.

As usual, she tried to see the bright side of the situation. This might all be for the best. She would probably hate having a husband who would no doubt want to tell her what to do every hour of the day, as some husbands did. She wasn't all that sure about sharing a bed with a man, anyway. From all she'd heard, which wasn't much, marital relations were messy and bothersome and perhaps only *occasionally* pleasurable. The act was for creating life and for a man's release. At least, that is what she'd taken from what she'd heard. To hear her married friends tell it, their husbands were quite disagreeable if they did not get their way in the bedroom. Not that they shared everything with her. Because she was an unmarried woman, they deemed some conversations unfit for her virginal ears.

For as long as Lyssa could remember, her father had been overly protective of his only child, shielding her from those he deemed unsavory or unsuitable and protecting her from the harshness of life. Sinmora had not prepared her stepdaughter for marriage, instead saying that it was a husband's place to instruct his bride as he saw fit. This statement was always followed by a flush of her cheeks and a quick turn away.

Lyssa didn't care. Not anymore. There would be no husband to instruct her. No conversations of intimate matters with married friends. Her life had taken a different turn. Lying in the dark she had to wonder... Had her prospective grooms met misfortune or loved another because she'd chosen them? Or had she chosen them because, in the deepest, darkest part of herself, she had somehow known what was to come? She didn't want to think that two men had died simply because she'd agreed to marry them. She preferred to think that she'd chosen them because they were meant to die. There was less weight on her conscience that way. If she possessed any magical abilities at all, that was the extent of it. What a worthless bit of magic *that* was!

She tried to convince herself that she would be fine, but silent tears fell from her eyes and slipped down her cheeks. While self-pity was not an attractive trait in anyone, she decided she deserved to feel sorry for herself, at least for one night. She would be strong tomorrow.

As she cried, her stomach growled. She shouldn't have skipped supper. Maybe there were a lot of "shouldn'ts" in her life, but at the moment that was the big one. She was hungry. This problem she could fix. Lyssa threw back the coverlet and left her bed, heading for the main room where earlier in the day she'd almost become a bride. The large room was used as a sitting area for family and for visitors, and in one corner there sat a stove and work space where meals were prepared. There was also a small table there, just right for three. As she headed for that table she thanked her lucky stars that this house also had two small but private bed chambers; one for her and one for her father and Sinmora. As she would apparently be living here for a very long time, having her own room—however small—was a luxury.

She and Kyran had decided to live here for a while after the wedding that hadn't been, but the plan had been to soon have a place of their own. Their own small house, their own kitchen. A home they could share, just the two of them, until babies started to arrive. And now…now she couldn't even imagine having her own home. It was such a simple desire. She did not wish for wealth or great beauty or power. Just a couple of rooms she could call her own.

Her father and stepmother were still awake, talking. She heard their muffled voices from beyond their closed bed chamber door as she uncovered a half loaf of bread.

She tried to be quiet as she cut a slice. There was no need to disturb them, and if they knew she was up and about they would probably feel obligated to attempt to soothe her. She did not wish to be soothed. She wished to wallow in misery for a while longer.

Their voices were low but carried well; *too* well as those voices rose slightly. She didn't try to listen, that would be rude, but a word caught her attention, and the knife she'd been wielding stopped moving mid-slice.

Baby.

Lyssa didn't move for a moment as her hand clenched on the handle of the knife. Her bare toes curled on the smooth wooden floor. Perhaps one of their friends was going to have a child, she reasoned. Sinmora was a few years younger than her husband and she had several younger acquaintances who had many children. Though it wasn't a subject they discussed openly with their daughter, Lyssa knew they had always wanted babies. It simply hadn't happened. Sinmora was nearly forty years old, far too old to have another child. Far too old.

More words drifted her way.

"Maybe it's a boy. You always wanted a son."

"You must be careful. I'm worried."

"When will we tell Lyssa?"

"Let's wait. She's had a difficult day, and this news will come as quite a shock."

Lyssa didn't breathe for a long moment.

"Cyrus, we must find her a proper husband."

Lyssa's knees went weak. She could no longer fool herself into thinking that they were talking about someone else. This house was about to become a bit crowded. Would she be sharing a room with the new baby, or would the child stay in the room where her parents slept? If the baby was a boy, her father would finally have a son to carry on his trade. She'd never realized that her father wanted a son so badly, that she was undoubtedly a disappointment simply because she was a girl. She should have known. Men always wanted sons.

Her already horrid day took an abrupt turn for the worse. She would be nothing but a burden, a daughter long past marriageable age who continued to live at home. Another mouth to feed, an old maid, an embarrassment to the family. No man would have her after four failed attempts at becoming a bride, and if the witch had been right, her window for marriage would close in mere hours. A nunnery was beginning to seem like a good idea.

In the near distance, bells rang, counting down the hours of the day. Each peal shot through her, and she held her breath as she silently counted. How many hours until she turned twenty-three? The peals ended and she held her breath. Two hours until midnight. Two hours until she turned twenty-three and all hope was lost.

Her heart leapt; her hands trembled. The witch had said her path was her own, that her future was in her hands. Did that mean there was something she could do about her current predicament? Could she save herself from a life of loneliness instead of feeling sorry for herself and waiting for someone else to save her?

Two hours to find a husband and take her vows. Two hours to become a wife, well and true. Wedded and bedded. Eight years ago she hadn't understood exactly what that meant. She was older now, and she even though she had not been well-instructed when it came to marital relations, she understood well enough.

A fresh thought occurred to her. She was to be married by twenty-three. There was nothing in the witch's prediction that said the husband she took before twenty-three would be her *only* husband. Maybe the *who* didn't matter at all, simply the time and date. Dissolution ceremonies were rare, but not unheard of. If she took a man as husband tonight strictly to fulfill the obligation to be a wife before her twenty-third birthday, maybe it would buy her some time to find the *right* man.

If the right man for her was out there. Somewhere.

Lyssa ran toward her bedchamber to dress. She had two hours to find a man and convince him to marry her. More accurately, two hours to marry and consummate the marriage. Vellance had been clear enough about that. She had to be a real wife before midnight.

All she needed was a willing man. Fortunately for her, any man would do.

* * * * * *

The Columbyana novels:
in order of publication:

The Sun Witch
The Moon Witch
The Star Witch

Prince of Magic
Prince of Fire
Prince of Swords

Untouchable
22 Nights
Bride by Command

Bride by Midnight

For a complete list of previous and upcoming releases
check here:
http://www.lindawinsteadjones.com

Linda Winstead Jones

Linda's first book, the historical romance *Guardian Angel*, was released in 1994, and in the years since she's written in several romance sub-genres under several names. In order of appearance, Linda Winstead; Linda Jones; Linda Winstead Jones; Linda Devlin; and Linda Fallon. She's a six time finalist for the RITA Award and a winner (for *Shades of Midnight*, writing as Linda Fallon) in the paranormal category. She's a *New York Times* and *USA Today* bestselling author of seventy books. Most recently she's been writing as Linda Jones in a couple of joint projects with Linda Howard, and rereleasing some of her backlist in ebook format. She can be found at any one of a variety of Facebook pages (search for Linda Winstead Jones and Linda Howard/Linda Jones) and at:
http://www.lindawinsteadjones.com.

Linda lives in Huntsville, Alabama. She can be reached at:
lindawinsteadjonesauthor@gmail.com

Twitter at @LWJbooks
https://twitter.com/LWJbooks

Facebook:
https://www.facebook.com/pages/Linda-Winstead-Jones/103936415079

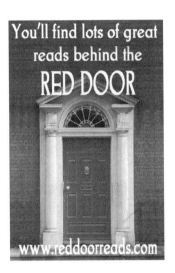

27812541R00048

Made in the USA
Charleston, SC
22 March 2014